The Little
Humpbacked Horse

The Little Humpbacked Horse

A Russian Tale

Adapted by Elizabeth Winthrop
Illustrated by Alexander Koshkin

Clarion Books/New York

Clarion Books
a Houghton Mifflin Company imprint
215 Park Avenue South, New York, NY 10003
Text copyright © 1997 by Elizabeth Winthrop
Illustrations copyright © 1997 by Alexander Koshkin

The illustrations for this book were executed in watercolor, tempera, and gouache.
The text for this book is set in 15/19-point Phaistos.

For information about this and other Houghton Mifflin trade and reference
books and multimedia products, visit The Bookstore at Houghton Mifflin
on the World Wide Web at (http://www.hmco.com/trade/).

Printed in Singapore.

Winthrop, Elizabeth.
The little humpbacked horse: a Russian tale / adapted by Elizabeth Winthrop ;
illustrated by Alexander Koshkin.
p.   cm.
Summary: A young peasant, with the help of his faithful horse, captures mag-
ical beasts, marries the woman he loves, and becomes the Tsar of Russia.
ISBN 0-395-65361-4
[1. Fairy tales.   2. Folklore—Russia.]   I. Koshkin, Alexander, ill.
II. Ershov, P. P. (Petr Pavlovich), 1815-1869.   Konek-gorbunok.   III. Title.
PZ8.W74Li   1997
398.2—dc20
[E]   95-43994
CIP
AC

TWP   10   9   8   7   6   5   4   3   2   1

To Charles de la Pasture, my cousin across the ocean.
—E. W.

With appreciation to Anne Diebel.
—A. K.

CHAPTER ONE

IN A LAND ACROSS THE OCEAN and beyond the high mountains, there once lived a peasant with three sons. Daniel, the first-born, was a clever young man. Gabriel, the middle one, was neither smart nor stupid. But Ivan, the youngest, was a simple boy who loved nothing better than to sleep away the days as well as the nights.

Early one morning the peasant discovered that a thief had come in the night and stolen hay from his haystack. So he ordered Daniel, his oldest and smartest son, to guard the haystack all through the night.

Snow lay thick in the fields and the night was bitter cold, so Daniel soon gave up the watch. He pulled his fur coat around him, crawled into a warm corner of the barn, and went to sleep.

When he woke up the next morning, he found that once again the thief had stolen hay from the stack. Clever Daniel rolled in the snow and returned home.

"Did you catch the thief?" his father asked.

"No, but when I heard him prowling I shouted so long and hard I scared him away!" Daniel answered. "Father, the night was bitterly cold and I am frozen to the bone."

The father praised his eldest and wisest son for his bravery, and on the second night he sent Gabriel to guard the haystack. On this night rain fell from the sky in great sheets.

"Father thinks my brother is the smart one," Gabriel said to himself, "but it seems stupid to sit out in the rain all night just to guard some old dried grass." So he found a sheltered spot and went to sleep.

And when, in the morning, he found that more hay had been stolen, he poured water from a nearby stream over his clothes and then went home.

"Did you catch the thief?" his father asked.

"I certainly did!" cried Gabriel. "I grabbed him and shook him, but in the end he slipped away from me. Look how wet I am, Father."

The peasant praised his second son for his courage, and that evening he sent his third son, Ivan, to guard the hay. "I don't know what good it will do," the peasant said to himself. "The boy is nothing but a simpleton."

The happy-go-lucky Ivan tucked a crust of bread under his coat and went out to the field. He did not sleep as his brothers had but marched from one corner of the field to the other, searching for the thief. And when he found no one, he sat down under the clear night sky and counted the stars while he munched on his bread.

Suddenly Ivan heard the whinnying of a horse. He peered out into the darkness and there stood a magnificent mare. She was as white as snow and her golden mane was curled into tiny ringlets.

As Ivan watched in amazement, the mare came closer and closer. When she was close enough to touch, Ivan grabbed her by the tail and jumped onto her back, wrong way around. The mare snorted with rage, and like an arrow she shot across the field, up one side of the mountain, then down the other, then deep into the forest. All the time she kept tossing her head from side to side, trying to shake the rider loose. But Ivan held on to her tail as tight as he could and stuck to her back like a burr.

When the sun rose, the mare finally stopped running. She spoke to Ivan in a human voice. "Since I cannot throw you off, Ivan," she panted, "I will make a deal with you. If you give me a place to rest for three nights and let me out each morning at sunrise to roll in the dewy grass, I will give you three colts. Two will be stallions fit for the Tsar. The third one will be a little humpbacked horse only three feet high with long ears. Don't ever part with him, for he will be your wisest counselor and keep you safe and warm for the rest of your days."

Ivan agreed. He hid the white mare in the shepherd's corral and went home to tell his brothers how he had ridden the thief all through the night. They only laughed at him and did not believe a word of his story.

CHAPTER TWO

$\mathcal{E}$VERY MORNING, just as he had promised, Ivan let the mare out to roll in the dewy grass. On the fourth day, she presented him with the three colts. Two were handsome brown-and-gray stallions with golden manes and pearl-studded hoofs. The third was the size of a tiny pony with long floppy ears and two humps on his back.

Then Ivan let the mare go free. She shot like an arrow across the field and disappeared from sight.

Ivan kept the horses in the corral, and he fed them, groomed them, and played with them. His favorite was the tiny humpbacked horse, who pranced about on his small hoofs and clapped his long floppy ears.

One night, Daniel stumbled into the old corral on his way home from an evening of carousing in the town. When he saw the horses, he ran to his brother Gabriel and dragged him back to the corral.

The brothers stared and stared at the two handsome stallions as they switched their golden tails and tossed their golden manes and pawed the ground with their pearl-studded hoofs.

"They say it takes a fool to find a treasure," said Daniel. "Now I know why Ivan spends so much time in this old corral."

"These are horses fit for a Tsar," Gabriel said. "Let's take them to the marketplace in the capital next week and sell them. We shall be rich and our simpleminded brother will never be the wiser."

The following week, the two brothers snuck into the corral after dark, rounded up the two magnificent horses, and headed for the capital.

The next morning when Ivan found his horses missing, he fell down on his knees and wept. The little humpbacked horse clapped his long ears and spoke to Ivan in a human voice. "Do not waste your time weeping, little Ivan. Your brothers have stolen the stallions. Get up on my back and grab my ears and I shall take you to them."

As soon as Ivan got up on his back, the little humpbacked horse shot like an arrow down the road. In no time at all they drew up next to those two thieving brothers.

"I may not be as clever as the two of you," Ivan cried. "But I have never stolen anything from you."

The two brothers raised their hands to the sky, protesting that they had only taken the stallions to help their poor father because of the terrible harvest. "And, little brother, we were planning to buy you a red cap and a pair of new boots with red heels."

"Really?" said Ivan. "In that case, I'll come with you."

On hearing this, Daniel and Gabriel wished to strangle their fool of a brother, but they had to take him along.

As soon as the high-stepping horses entered the marketplace, the people pressed around to admire them. The Tsar's own groom was one of the crowd. When he saw the brown-and-gray stallions, he rushed back to the palace to tell the Tsar.

The moment the Tsar heard the man's excited babblings, he called for his state carriage and rode to the market.

"How much do you want for them?" he asked Ivan.

"Fifteen caps full of silver and a five-ruble gold piece too," said Ivan.

"You shall have it," said the Tsar, and ordered the money to be handed over.

But when the Tsar's ten grooms came to lead the horses away, the stallions bit right through their bridles and galloped back to Ivan.

"It seems that these horses will obey only you," said the Tsar to Ivan. "Very well then, you must come along too. I will make you my new Master of the Stables."

The happy Ivan gave his brothers all the money and told them to take it to their father. Then he led the two horses to the royal stables. The little humpbacked horse pranced along beside Ivan and would not be parted from him.

CHAPTER THREE

$\mathscr{I}$VAN HAD A FINE TIME as Master of the Stables. He wore red shiny boots and ate all the food he wanted. Every morning he took the horses to roll in the dew in the open field, and he fed them honey and wheat and brushed their coats until they shone.

But the more the Tsar praised his new Master of the Stables, the more jealous others grew. Finally there came a time when the Tsar could no longer ignore the whisperings. He called together his courtiers and asked them what was the matter.

Now the Tsar was a rich man but a greedy one, and no matter how many treasures he possessed he always wanted more. For years he had longed to own the Sow with Golden Bristles and Silver Tusks and her twenty sucklings, but he did not have the courage or the cunning to trap this magical beast.

So when the Tsar asked for an explanation, the courtiers knew just what to say. One of them stepped forward and, with a false and sorrowful face, told the Tsar that the new Master of the Stables was an evil sorcerer. "He has bragged to us that he could find the Sow with Golden Bristles and Silver Tusks and bring her to you along with her twenty sucklings. And, Your Majesty, nobody has ever been able to do that for you."

The Tsar was angry. He ordered Ivan to do as he had boasted within three days or his life would be worth nothing. Ivan ran to tell the little humpbacked horse of his misfortune.

"Don't upset yourself, Ivan," the little horse said softly. "Go to the Tsar and ask him for three things: a bucket of golden wheat, a bucket of silver barley, and a silk rope."

When Ivan returned the humpbacked horse said, "Lie down and sleep now, Ivan. Things always look better in the morning."

When the sun rose, Ivan climbed on the back of his little horse and they dashed away across the wide plains and over the mountains. Finally they reached a deep valley at the edge of a dark wood.

The little humpbacked horse told Ivan to pour the wheat in one pile and the barley in another, and then to hide and wait. As the evening shadows fell across the valley, Ivan heard scuffling and grunting. Before long, he spied the Sow with Golden Bristles and Silver Tusks leading her twenty sucklings out of the forest. She rushed over to the wheat, but the baby pigs stopped to eat the silver barley. Ivan sprang from his hiding place and tied the sucklings one by one with his silken rope, then wound the end of the rope around the horn of the saddle. He jumped on the horse's back and the little humpbacked horse sped away like an arrow. When the sow saw that her sucklings were being taken from her, she ran after them all the way to the capital.

The Tsar was so delighted to see that his Master of the Stables had granted his dearest wish, he rewarded Ivan with rich gifts and praised him to one and all. Once again, the jealous courtiers whispered together, searching for a way to destroy Ivan.

CHAPTER FOUR

*I*N A FEW DAYS, the courtiers came again before the Tsar. They told him that Ivan was now boasting that he could bring the Tsar the Magnificent Mare with Seven Manes and her seven fierce stallions. Once again the greedy Tsar believed them. He ordered the bewildered Ivan to go immediately to the emerald green meadow nestled between the crystal hills of the Caucasus and bring back the priceless mare and her seven stallions. "And if you fail to do as I command in seven days," the Tsar thundered, "your life will not be worth living."

Once again Ivan ran to tell his trusted companion. The little humpbacked horse consoled him. "Don't trouble yourself, Ivan. Ask the Tsar to build a stone stable with one door opening into it and one opening out. Ask him also for a horse's hide and an iron hammer weighing forty pounds."

Ivan did all these things, and when he returned the little hump-backed horse said, "Lie down and sleep now, Ivan, for remember, life seems sweeter in the morning."

When the day broke, Ivan mounted his little humpbacked horse and for three days and three nights they flew like the wind until they reached the emerald green meadow between the crystal hills.

"Now sew me into the hide," the little humpbacked horse commanded. "When the mare attacks me, strike her between the ears with the hammer to stun her. Then jump onto my back, and you will be able to lead her along after me. Her seven stallions will follow."

Ivan did everything the little humpbacked horse told him, and sure enough, he soon captured the mare. The seven stallions thundered along after her, all the way back to the Tsar's capital.

Ivan rode right into the stone stable with the mare and her seven stallions following. Quickly he barred both doors so they could not escape, and then he went straight to the Tsar.

Once again, the Tsar was mightily pleased and praised his stablemaster. The jealous courtiers were beside themselves with fury and plotted again to destroy Ivan.

Chapter Five

Soon the courtiers came again before the Tsar. They said, "Your Majesty, the stablemaster tells all he meets that to capture the mare and her seven stallions was a simple chore. Now he brags that he can bring you the greatest treasure of all, the beautiful Tsarevna who rows her golden boat with the silver oars. Everyone in the kingdom knows that you have long wished to make her your bride. He is making a fool of you."

At this, the Tsar rose up in great wrath and once more ordered Ivan brought before him. "I command you to go at once across three times nine lands and bring to me the beautiful Tsarevna. If you do not do as I say within twelve days, I shall cut off your head."

When the little humpbacked horse heard his master's tale of woe, he licked Ivan's hand with his tiny rough tongue. "This is not so difficult a task," he said. "Tell the Tsar you need two tablecloths embroidered in gold, a silken tent woven with golden thread, and also gold and silver plates, sweet wines, and tasty delicacies."

When Ivan brought all these things to the stable, his little humpbacked horse urged him to sleep away his troubles and reminded him once again that the world always seems brighter in

the morning. As soon as the sun rose, Ivan mounted the little humpbacked horse, and they sped away like the wind.

At the end of six days and six nights they reached the very edge of the world, where the orange sun rises out of the blue ocean. There Ivan pitched the tent on the warm white sand. He placed the tasty sweet dishes on the two tablecloths inside. Then he hid behind the tent and, as the little humpbacked horse had directed, he watched through a tiny hole in the silk for the Tsarevna to come.

Soon Ivan heard the creak of the silver oars on the golden boat. When the boat reached the shore, the Tsarevna stepped out onto the warm white sand and looked inside the tent. The moment she saw the wine and the tasty dishes, she sat down and ate and drank until she was full. Ivan was so taken by her beauty that he forgot what he was supposed to do. He was still gazing at her in wonder when she slipped out of the tent and sailed away in her golden boat.

Ivan was filled with shame that he had failed. "She will be back again tomorrow," the little humpbacked horse told him. "But this will be your last chance."

The next day Ivan once again spread out the wines and sweets to tempt the Tsarevna. And this time when she came he threw his arms around her and called out for his faithful horse. When the Tsarevna saw Ivan's handsome face, she stopped struggling, and he was able to lift her easily into the saddle. And as soon as the little humpbacked horse felt the weight of the two of them on his back, he made his way back down the road toward the capital.

They rode for six days and six nights, but Ivan and the Tsarevna barely noticed because they had fallen so deeply in love with each other. On the seventh day, they arrived at the palace. With a sad face and a heavy heart, Ivan handed the beautiful maiden over to the Tsar.

CHAPTER SIX

THE TSAR WAS OVERJOYED. The Tsarevna was even more beautiful than he had imagined. He took her by the hand and vowed that she would be his bride.

But the Tsarevna turned away from him. "You are an old man past sixty," she said. "People will laugh when they see that the Tsar has married a girl young enough to be his granddaughter."

The Tsar did everything he could to change her mind, but the Tsarevna merely shook her head. "I will not marry a man with gray hair," she said. "However, when you become young again, I will happily marry you."

"How can a man grow young again?" asked the Tsar.

"I have heard that it is possible, but it takes a very brave man," said the Tsarevna.

"Simply tell me what to do and I will do it," the Tsar pleaded.

"Order three large caldrons to be set out in the palace court-yard," said the girl. "Fill the first with boiling mares' milk, the second with boiling water, and the third with cold water. He who jumps into the boiling milk, then into the boiling water, and then into the cold water will become young again and handsome beyond words. If you do that, then I shall become your Tsaritsa."

When the jealous courtiers heard this, they gathered around the Tsar. "Surely, sire, no human being can throw himself into boiling liquid and live. Send for the Master of the Stables to take the test first."

The Tsar agreed that this was wise advice and sent for Ivan. When Ivan heard what he was to do, he threw himself down before the little humpbacked horse and cried, "O, my most faithful friend, you have helped me find the Sow with Golden Bristles and the Mare with Seven Manes and best of all, the beautiful Tsarevna, but nothing will save me from this terrible fate. I am about to be boiled to death like a chicken."

"Do not weep, my dear master," said the little humpbacked horse. "For I have a plan to save you. Tell the Tsar that you wish me brought to you. As soon as I come into the courtyard, I will gallop three times around the three caldrons, dip my tail in each, and sprinkle you. Then instantly you must jump into and out of each caldron, one right after the other."

The three caldrons were set out in the center of the palace courtyard. When the Tsar's soldiers led Ivan into the courtyard, he bowed low before the Tsar and begged to be allowed to see his little humpbacked horse one last time. As soon as the little horse came prancing into the courtyard, he galloped three times around the caldrons, dipped his tail into each one, and sprinkled his master. Ivan instantly stripped off his clothes and jumped first into the boiling mares' milk, then into the boiling water, and finally into the cold water. And when he stood up and shook off the last drops of cold water, he was even more handsome than before.

When the Tsar saw what had happened to Ivan, he did not even bother to undress but leaped headlong into the boiling milk. And in a single instant he was scalded to death.

Once the people saw what had happened to the Tsar, they looked to Ivan for guidance. He brought forward the Tsarevna, who held her hands up for silence. "Your Tsar chose me to be his Tsaritsa and help him rule," she said. "Now that he is gone, I wish to marry the brave and handsome Ivan."

The people were pleased, for the Tsar had been a greedy ruler. They shouted and stamped their feet and called out, "Health to Tsar Ivan!"

So the two were married and held a great feast. All the people were invited, and the music played long into the night. Even the nasty courtiers who had plotted against Ivan drank and ate and danced for so long that they could barely stand at the end of it.

Ivan, with his Tsaritsa, ruled the land wisely and well. And the little humpbacked horse stayed close by Ivan's side, for he was Ivan's most faithful and loving friend and his wisest counselor.

Author's Note

As is often true in Russian folktales, the characters in *The Little Humpbacked Horse* surprise us. Simple fools turn out to be heroes, wisdom is delivered by strange messengers, and a princess takes an active role in her own fate. The happy-go-lucky Ivan seems to be a simpleton, but in his innocence he exposes first his dishonest brothers and then the greedy Tsar and his jealous courtiers. The heroes in these fairy tales inevitably have a helper; in this one, Ivan is walked through each of his seemingly impossible tasks by an unlikely looking counselor, a tiny little humpbacked horse. In Russian folklore, the women usually turn out to be more than pretty princesses; this Tsarevna proves to be a strong-willed young woman who knows how to keep her wits about her.

For me, the particular charm of this tale lies in the still, small voice of the little humpbacked horse that talks Ivan through his wild and often frightening forays to capture magical beasts and in the end, an equally magical princess.

—Elizabeth Winthrop